BOOKS WRITTEN BY **KATE KLISE**
ILLUSTRATED BY **M. SARAH KLISE**

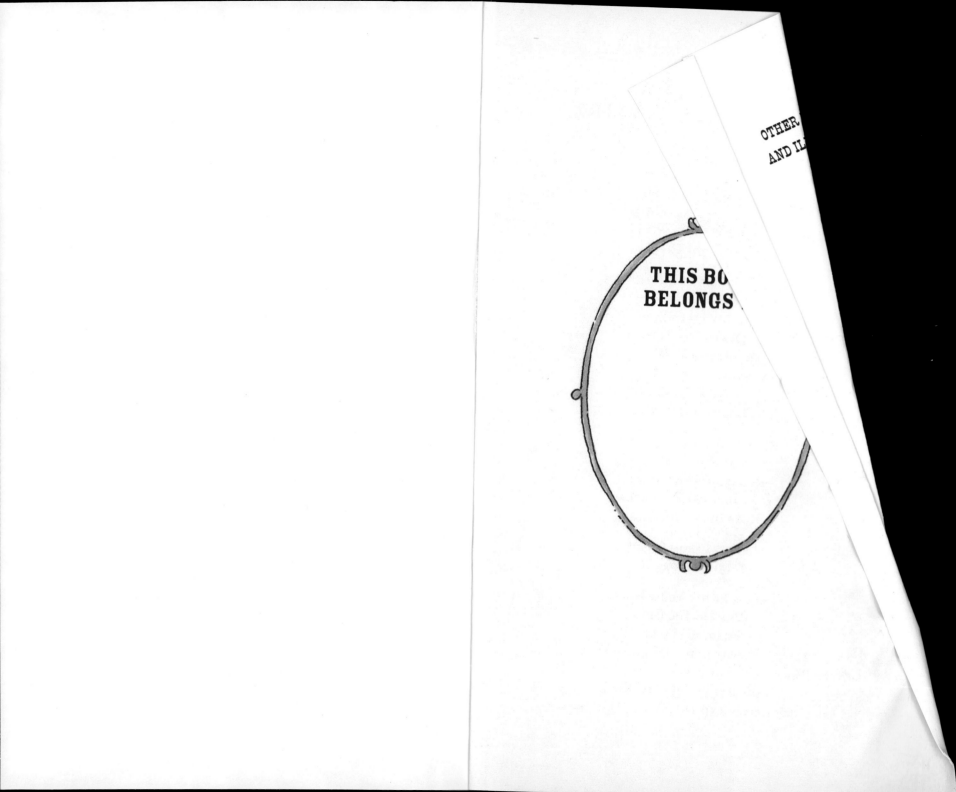

OTHER
AND IL

THIS BO
BELONGS

BOOK 5
Three-Ring
Rascals

SECRETS
of the
CIRCUS

KATE KLISE

ILLUSTRATED BY
M. SARAH KLISE

ALGONQUIN YOUNG READERS • 2016

Published by
Algonquin Young Readers
An imprint of Algonquin Books of Chapel Hill
P.O. Box 2225
Chapel Hill, NC 27514

a division of
Workman Publishing
225 Varick Street
New York, New York 10014

LIBRARY OF CONGRESS CATALOGING-IN-PUBLICATION DATA
Names: Klise, Kate, author. | Klise, M. Sarah, illustrator. | Klise, Kate. Three-ring rascals ; bk. 5.
Title: Secrets of the circus / Kate Klise ; illustrated by M. Sarah Klise.
Description: First edition. | Chapel Hill, North Carolina : Algonquin Young Readers, 2016. |
Series: Three-ring rascals ; book 5 | Summary: "The animals of Sir Sidney's Circus enter a
contest at the Iowa State Fair in hopes of winning a $5,000 prize that could save Farmer
Farley's farm and his prize pig, Pablo"— Provided by publisher.
Identifiers: LCCN 2015034263 | ISBN 9781616205669
Subjects: LCSH: Circus—Juvenile fiction. | Pen pals—Juvenile fiction. | Conduct of life—
Juvenile fiction. | CYAC: Circus—Fiction. | Pen pals—Fiction. | Conduct of life—Fiction.
Classification: LCC PZ7.K684 Se 2016 | DDC [Fic]—dc23
LC record available at http://lccn.loc.gov/2015034263

10 9 8 7 6 5 4 3 2 1
First Edition

This book is dedicated to
pen pals everywhere.

BOOK 5
Three-Ring Rascals

SECRETS
of the
CIRCUS

Do nothing secretly;
for Time sees and hears all things, and discloses all.
—Sophocles

❧CHAPTER ONE❧

Old Coal was no ordinary crow. She was a member of Sir Sidney's Circus, the best circus in the whole wide world. Her job was to deliver mail to and from the circus train.

Now that Old Coal was getting older, she needed glasses to read the names and numbers on the envelopes.

Old Coal always wore her glasses, except when she was sleeping. Then she kept them on a table next to her bed.

But one morning, Old Coal woke up to find her glasses were gone.

Nearby in a mouse hole, Bert was also waking up. He was one of two mice who traveled around the country with Sir Sidney's Circus. Now that he was getting older, Bert liked to spend a few minutes every morning working on his diary. He enjoyed writing about his life as a circus mouse.

But Bert couldn't write in his diary on that sunny morning because he couldn't find his favorite pen.

"Gert," he said to his sister, "have you seen my favorite pen? I thought for sure I put it in my pocket."

"No," Gert said. "I haven't seen your pen. Have you seen my necklace? I could have sworn I put it on the piano."

But the necklace wasn't there.

A lot of things were missing that day on Sir Sidney's Circus train. Leo the lion couldn't find his bow tie.

Tiger the kitten couldn't find her favorite ball of string.

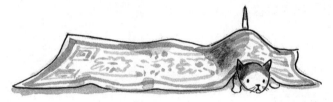

Elsa the elephant was missing her headband.

The Famous Flying Banana Brothers were missing two comic books.

And Sir Sidney, who owned the circus, was missing his favorite cuff links.

Just then, Sir Sidney heard a noise.

The noise was coming from Sir Sidney's desk.
Sir Sidney bent down to look under it. There was nothing
but a little dust.

The noise continued. *Squeak. Squeak. Squeak.*

"What is making that noise?" Sir Sidney said to
himself. He opened the bottom drawer.

That's when he saw her. A pack rat had moved into
Sir Sidney's desk and was building a nest out of stolen
treasures.

An hour later, Sir Sidney called a meeting. "I'd like to introduce you all to Ruby," he said.

Everyone stared in disbelief.

Stan Banana pointed to the rat's nest. "Are *those* our comic books?" he asked.

"That rat chewed them to shreds!" added Dan Banana.

"Look what you've done to Elsa's headband," said Leo.

"You've destroyed Leo's bow tie," said Elsa.

"Mrrare mrrare," purred Tiger sadly. She used her tail to point to what was once her favorite ball of string.

"Why did you chew up everyone's stuff?" asked Bert.

"It's my nature," said Ruby without apology. "I like to chew. Besides, I needed material to build my nest."

"But surely you didn't need my necklace or Bert's favorite pen," said Gert. "And aren't those Sir Sidney's cuff links and Old Coal's glasses?"

"I like shiny things," said Ruby, shrugging.

"Well, *we* don't like thieves!" said Bert. "Or sneaks."

"Aw! Aw!" agreed Old Coal, who swooped down to retrieve her glasses.

"Sir Sidney," said Leo, "tell Ruby that we don't like anyone stealing our things and hiding them in a secret place."

Anger was in the air. All the circus performers felt it. But instead of getting mad at Ruby, Sir Sidney made a surprising announcement.

"Everyone has a secret," said Sir Sidney. "Tonight after dinner, let's talk about our secrets. Maybe we'll learn something about ourselves and our friends."

So that night, they shared their secrets.

Gert said nothing.

"It's your turn, Gert," said Leo. "What's your secret?"

"Tell us," said Elsa.

But Gert shook her little head. "My secret is more serious than any of yours," she said. Her whiskers trembled as she spoke.

"That's not fair," said Leo. "We told you our secrets. Now you have to tell us yours."

"I'd rather not," said Gert. She was now nibbling her claws.

"Oh, come on," said Elsa. "Just *tell* us. You have to

tell us. Isn't that right, Sir Sidney?"

"Gert doesn't have to share her secret if she doesn't want to," said Sir Sidney. "It's late. We've all had a long day. Time for bed."

Gert's whiskers were still quivering as she lay in bed.

"Gee," said Bert, climbing under the covers of his bed, "I can't believe you wouldn't tell everyone your secret." Then he lowered his voice to a whisper. "But you can tell *me*. I won't tell anyone."

"Because," insisted Gert, "you wouldn't understand."

Their conversation was interrupted by a sharp jerking motion and the sound of a loud squeal coming from the front of the train.

EEEEEEEE!

"The Banana brothers must be slamming on the brakes," said Bert. He raced with Gert to the engine car to see why the train had stopped so suddenly. When the mice arrived, they found everyone else there, too. Leo was holding his paws over his ears to muffle the loud noise.

"Why is the train still squealing if we've come to a complete stop?" Bert asked.

"It's not the train," said Stan Banana.

"Look," said Dan Banana. He pointed outside to a pig who was standing on the tracks and crying.

"That's my secret," said Gert softly. "His name is Pablo."

CHAPTER TWO

Gert explained everything the next day.

"Pablo and I are pen pals," she said. "We met through an ad in the *Circus Times*." Gert showed everyone the ad.

LOOKING FOR A PEN PAL?

Write a note with a pencil or pen.
We'll match you with a new best friend!

The Pen Pal Shop
P.O. Box 744
Mountain Grove, MO 65711

"You've been pen pals with a *pig*?" said Bert. "Why didn't you tell us?"

"It was my secret," said Gert. "Old Coal delivered our letters. She's the only one who knew."

"From your ink pen to his pig pen," said Sir Sidney.

"Actually," said Pablo, "Gert didn't use a pen to write her letters. She used a typewriter. It's a marvelous little machine. The *i* key sometimes sticks, but other than that, it's perfect."

Yeah, I know. Gert is my sister.

She's my friend.

Mine, too.

Well, Gert is my friend and my hero. You might say she's my *frero*.

friend + hero = frero

Pablo likes to make up words, too!

"Why is Gert your hero—or *frero*?" asked Sir Sidney.

"Because she saved my life," said Pablo.

"I *did*?" asked Gert. "How?"

Pablo lowered his snout so he could speak directly to Gert. "Your letters convinced me to escape," he said. "I ran away from the farm yesterday, just like you said I should. Now Farmer Farley can't sell me to Prinkle's Pork Chops."

I couldn't bear the thought of you being turned into pork chops.

Bert was confused. "How did you find the circus train?" he asked the pig.

"Gert sent me a map, along with your touring schedule," said Pablo. "She also sent me this shiny compass." He handed the compass to Gert.

"Did someone say 'shiny compass'?" asked Ruby. The pack rat was strolling by, looking for decorations to add to her nest. She helped herself to the compass Gert was holding.

"Ruby," said Sir Sidney firmly, "I don't allow anyone on my circus train to borrow things without permission. Please return everything you've taken, beginning with Gert's compass."

Ruby put her paws on her hips and cleared her throat.

Forgive me for asking, but do you know anything about pack rats?

No.

"I didn't think so," said Ruby. "Let me explain. Pack rats take things without asking. This is what we *do*. We also chew things to shreds."

"I understand," said Sir Sidney. "But I still want you to give back everything you've taken."

Ruby gaped at Sir Sidney. "Are you going to make the mouse give back the pig?"

"What do you mean?" asked Sir Sidney.

"He doesn't belong on this train," said Ruby, pointing at Pablo. "He belongs to a farmer. But he was lured here by a clever little mouse. In some counties, that's considered pig rustling."

"You mean *stealing*?" said Elsa.

"Gert's not a thief," said Leo.

"I'm not!" squeaked Gert. "I didn't *steal* Pablo. He came here because he wanted to."

"Do you or do you not have something that doesn't belong to you?" Ruby asked. She sounded like a police officer or a lawyer.

Gert looked into Pablo's big eyes.

"I guess I did encourage him to run away," she admitted. "But only because he was in danger. I didn't know I was doing something wrong."

"*Ignorantia juris non excusat*," said Ruby. "That's Latin for 'Ignorance of the law does not excuse.' Wrong is wrong, whether you know it or not."

Wow. How'd you get so smart?

I'm a reader. Pack rats are curious by nature.

"Pablo," said Sir Sidney, "how will Farmer Farley feel when he finds out you ran away?"

"He won't be happy," Pablo said. "I was his only pig. But I left Farmer Farley a letter. He's probably reading it right now."

Sure enough, twenty miles away, Farmer Farley was reading Pablo's letter.

August 12

Dear Farmer Farley,
      I know you want to sell me to Prinkle's Pork Chops. But I want to *live.* So I'm running away from the farm. I wish you all the luck in the world. Good-bye.

      Your friend and (former) pig,

      Pablo

When Farmer Farley finished reading the letter, he didn't shake his fist or say angry words. He didn't even stomp his feet.

No, what Farmer Farley did instead was cry. Why? Because he was broke. He had no money. Even worse, he owed five thousand dollars to Prinkle's Pork Chops.

That was Farmer Farley's secret.

❧ CHAPTER THREE ❧

The headquarters of Prinkle's Pork Chops looked like a silver birthday cake on the horizon. Smokestacks sat on top of the building like candles, belching big bursts of pork-scented smoke.

Inside, Penelope Prinkle, the owner and president of Prinkle's Pork Chops, sat at her desk, thinking about business. She was the richest person in Iowa. She often lent money to farmers, but only if she was sure they couldn't pay her back. When they didn't, she took their farms.

Penelope Prinkle kept notes on every farmer who owed her money. She smiled when she turned to Farmer Farley's page in her notebook.

Name:	Fred Farley
Owes me:	$5,000
Money due:	August 17, 3:00 p.m.
Or else:	I get his farm.

Penelope Prinkle knew Farmer Farley had only one pig, Pablo. "Farmer Farley will have to sell Pablo to repay his debt," she said to herself. "But how much would Pablo have to weigh to be worth five thousand dollars?"

Penelope Prinkle created a chart based on the price she paid for pigs: ten dollars per pound.

PRICE CHART FOR PIGS

WEIGHT (in pounds)	PRICE (at $10 per pound)
100	$1,000
200	$2,000
300	$3,000
400	$4,000
500	$5,000
600	$6,000
700	$7,000
800	$8,000
900	$9,000
1,000	$10,000

Pablo would have to weigh five hundred pounds to be worth five thousand dollars.

From her office window, Penelope Prinkle had spent years watching Pablo grow up. Fred Farley's farm was next door to Prinkle's Pork Chops. That was why Penelope Prinkle wanted his land.

Penelope Prinkle was pretty sure Pablo didn't weigh five hundred pounds. Even as a piglet, Pablo loved to run around the farm. Exercise made him lean rather than fat.

"If Pablo weighs less than five hundred pounds, I won't have to pay Farmer Farley five thousand dollars," Penelope Prinkle said to herself. "Farmer Farley won't be able to repay his loan, and his farm will belong to me."

She looked at her calendar. "Today is Thursday," she said. "At three o'clock on Sunday, Fred Farley's farm will be mine."

Penelope Prinkle smiled again. Oh, how she loved making money! She loved making money more than anything on earth.

That was her secret.

Back on the circus train, Bert was still trying to make sense of Gert's relationship with Pablo.

"Hogwash!" said Bert, rolling his eyes. "Don't you know pigs are the filthiest creatures on earth?"

"That's *not* true," said Gert. "Pigs aren't filthy. They roll around in the mud to keep cool."

"A stick in the mud like him should *stick* in the mud," said Bert.

Pablo's snout suddenly appeared in the mouse hole. "Gert? Oh, Gertie? Can you come out and play?"

"I'll be right there," Gert answered sweetly. She tied a scarf around her furry head and scurried out of the mouse hole.

Bert felt left out.

Ruby the rat had been listening outside the mouse hole. "There's no law that says you can't have a pen pal, too," she whispered.

"I don't *want* a pen pal," Bert said. "I have *lots* of friends. Everybody on this train is my friend. I have a really good friend named Flora who lives on a ship. I have another friend named Barnabas Brambles. He helped Sir Sidney run the circus for a while."

Bert showed Ruby a photo album of all his friends.

Ruby flipped through the pages. "You have a lot of friends," she said. "But I don't see you writing letters to any of them."

Bert sighed.

"Please *don't*," said Bert, grabbing the album back from Ruby. "Can't you quit chewing stuff?"

The idea had never occurred to Ruby. "I suppose I could *try* to quit," she said. "But only if *you'll* quit being so grouchy."

"I could try," said Bert. "But I really want a pen pal."

"Then do what Gert and Pablo did," said Ruby. "Send a letter to the Pen Pal Shop."

Bert snapped his claws. "That's a great idea!"

He grabbed his second-favorite pen. Ruby still had his favorite one. Then he dashed off a note.

PEN PAL WANTED

I'm looking for someone to send me letters.
I'll write back when I can.
Must like jokes, popcorn, and mice.

Bert the Mouse

Bert put the note in an envelope and gave it to
Old Coal to deliver.

Meanwhile, Elsa and Leo were in the dining car, sharing a milk shake and watching Gert and Pablo play.

Who needs a pen pal when I have a best friend like you?

Or you.

"But I'm happy Gert has found a new friend," said Leo. "She and Pablo look funny together, don't they? Gert is so tiny, and Pablo weighs almost as much as you!"

Elsa stopped sipping the shake. "I beg your pardon."

"Well, you weigh *more* than Pablo, of course," said Leo, before taking a big slurp of the milk shake.

"Of course I weigh more," said Elsa without smiling. "I'm an *elephant*. I'm supposed to be heavy. It's my nature. At least I've never had lice. Or fleas."

Leo stopped slurping. "I'm a *cat*. It's my nature to attract fleas."

Disgusting.

Is that any way to talk to your best friend?

"Maybe I need a *new* best friend who won't make fun of my weight," said Elsa.

"I wasn't making fun of your weight," said Leo. "You're the one who called *me* disgusting."

"I didn't call *you* disgusting," said Elsa. "I was talking about fleas. Oh, never mind. Where's that ad for the Pen Pal Shop? I'm going to write a letter and find a *new* best friend."

"I think I'll do the same thing," said Leo.

Leo and Elsa went to opposite ends of the train to write their letters.

LEO THE LION
Proud Member of Sir Sidney's Circus

August 14

Dear Pen Pal Shop,

I'm a nice lion who would never hurt anyone's feelings on purpose, especially not my best friend's feelings. Can you please help me find a new best friend?

Leo

From the Desk of Elsa

August 14

Dear Sir or Madam,

I am a healthy-sized elephant and am offering my friendship to anyone who can be a true friend in return. I had a best friend once. We had lots of laughs together until we started fighting. It's hard to stop fighting once you start.

Sincerely,

Elsa

Leo and Elsa gave their letters to Old Coal to deliver.

When the crow returned later that evening, she was carrying a newspaper. Sir Sidney had asked Old Coal to find the latest edition of the *New Pork Times*. He wanted to learn more about Pablo's situation.

THE NEW PORK TIMES

"All the pork that's fit to print with news that's never boaring"

Thursday, August 14 ✦ **50 cents** ✦ **Afternoon Edition**

Will Farmer Farley Keep His Farm?

Farmer Farley was planning to repay his $5,000 loan to Penelope Prinkle by selling his only pig, Pablo. But now that Pablo has run away, it seems unlikely that Farmer Farley will be able to come up with the money he needs to save his 40-acre farm.

"I can't believe Pablo ran away," said Farmer Farley. "I always treated him well. I made sure his pen was comfortable. I fed him as much corn as he wanted."

Some might say that Farmer Farley was generous to Pablo because he was trying to fatten him up to sell to Penelope Prinkle.

But Farmer Farley says that's not true. "I loved Pablo. I would give

Farmer Farley doesn't know how he will repay loan.

anything to be able to keep my pig and my farm, but I don't see how I can keep either one now that Pablo is gone. Maybe he'll come home."

Fat chance of that.

Pig Business Is Big Business

Some businesses slump during the hot summer months. Not Prinkle's Pork Chops.

"Profits are higher than ever," said owner Penelope Prinkle with a twinkle in her eye. "People enjoy eating pork chops year-round, but there's something special about a grilled pork chop on a summer night. Who can eat just one?"

Penelope Prinkle looks forward to expanding her business when she acquires Farmer Farley's land. "I haven't decided what I'll do with his 40 acres," she said. "But don't worry. I'll figure out the best way to make the most money for me."

Penelope Prinkle lives high on the hog.

Pig Race Will Take Place on Last Day of Fair

Come one, come all to the annual pig race at the Iowa State Fair, where the winning pig will take home a $5,000 cash prize.

Last year's winner, Sassy Sausage, is scheduled to run again in this year's race, which will begin at 2:30 P.M. on Sunday, August 17, the last day of the fair. Any Iowa pig is eligible to run. Applications will be accepted in advance by mail or on the day of the race.

Sassy Sausage will compete again in this year's race.

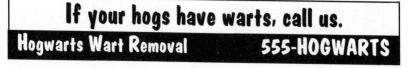

Sir Sidney put down the newspaper and began to pace.
Whenever he had something serious to think about,
Sir Sidney liked to walk.

On one hand, Pablo wants to be free.

On the other hand, Farmer Farley wants to keep his farm. How can he do that if he doesn't sell Pablo to Penelope Prinkle?

Sir Sidney tried to see all sides of every situation.
It helped him to find the best solution. "The bottom line,"
Sir Sidney said to himself, "is that Farmer Farley needs
five thousand dollars to save his farm."

Sir Sidney picked up the newspaper again and reread the article about the pig race. When he finished reading, he called Gert and Pablo to his office.

"Pablo," Sir Sidney said, "are you fast on your feet?"

"Yes, sir," said Pablo. "I love to run."

Sir Sidney explained that a pig race would take place on Sunday at the Iowa State Fair. "If Pablo wins the race," Sir Sidney said, "he'll get five thousand dollars."

"I could give the money to Farmer Farley!" Pablo said. "He could keep his farm, and I could have my freedom."

It's the perfect solution!

It's the *perfolution.*

perfect + solution = perfolution

The happy pen pals danced together in a circle, with Gert perched on Pablo's snout.

"Now there's a scene that will make you smile," Ruby said to Bert.

But Bert didn't feel like smiling. He felt lonely. He wished he had a pen pal.

That was Bert's secret.

❧ CHAPTER FOUR ❧

On Friday, Farmer Farley woke up in a terrible mood. He had also seen the article in the *New Pork Times*. His secret was out. Now everyone knew he was in debt.

"It's no fun being poor," Farmer Farley said to himself. "I can't go out to eat at nice restaurants. I can't buy gas for my tractor to harvest the corn. I can't even afford to go to the state fair this year."

Farmer Farley loved the Iowa State Fair. In the old days, when he had more money, he went to the fair every summer. He always ate his fill of funnel cakes and cotton candy. In fact, most years Farmer Farley made a pig of himself at the state fair.

I made a pig of myself, Farmer Farley thought.

A strange idea began to take shape in Farmer Farley's desperate mind. He picked up his copy of the *New Pork Times* and reread the story about the pig race.

"The winning pig will take home a five-thousand-dollar cash prize," he said again to himself. It was the *exact* amount he needed to save his farm.

He looked in the mirror. Could he *really* make a pig of himself?

It was worth a shot! He filled out the application, using the name Fat Chance.

PIG RACE OFFICIAL ENTRY FORM

Pig's name: _____Fat Chance_____

Owner's name: ___Fred Farley_____

Farm name: _____Farley Farm_____

Farmer Farley then pulled out his sewing machine and began to make a pig costume.

When he finished sewing, he created a training schedule for himself.

DIET	EXERCISE	POSITIVE THINKING	SLEEP
Protein Healthy fats Fruits and vegetables Whole grains	Run and lift weights.	"I'm the fastest pig alive." Repeat 100 times.	8 hours each night

"I don't have much time to get in shape," Farmer Farley said as he ran laps around his cornfield. "The pig race is the day after tomorrow."

As Penelope Prinkle watched from her window at
Prinkle's Pork Chops, she remembered that the annual
pig race at the Iowa State Fair was scheduled for Sunday.
She always enjoyed watching the silly event. Sometimes
she found farmers willing to sell their losing pigs for a low
price. She made a note to attend the pig race.

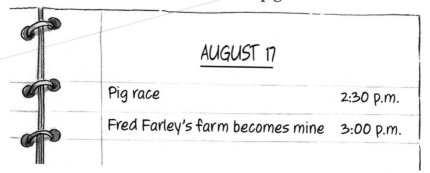

The next day on the circus train, everyone wanted to help Pablo train for the big pig race.

The Famous Flying Banana Brothers shared a lesson about balance.

Elsa focused on weight training.

Sir Sidney prepared a healthful meal for everyone.
"It feels good to eat food that's good for you," he said.

While they were eating, Old Coal delivered the day's mail.

"Look," said Leo, "a letter from the Pen Pal Shop!"

"I got one, too!" said Elsa.

They read their letters separately.

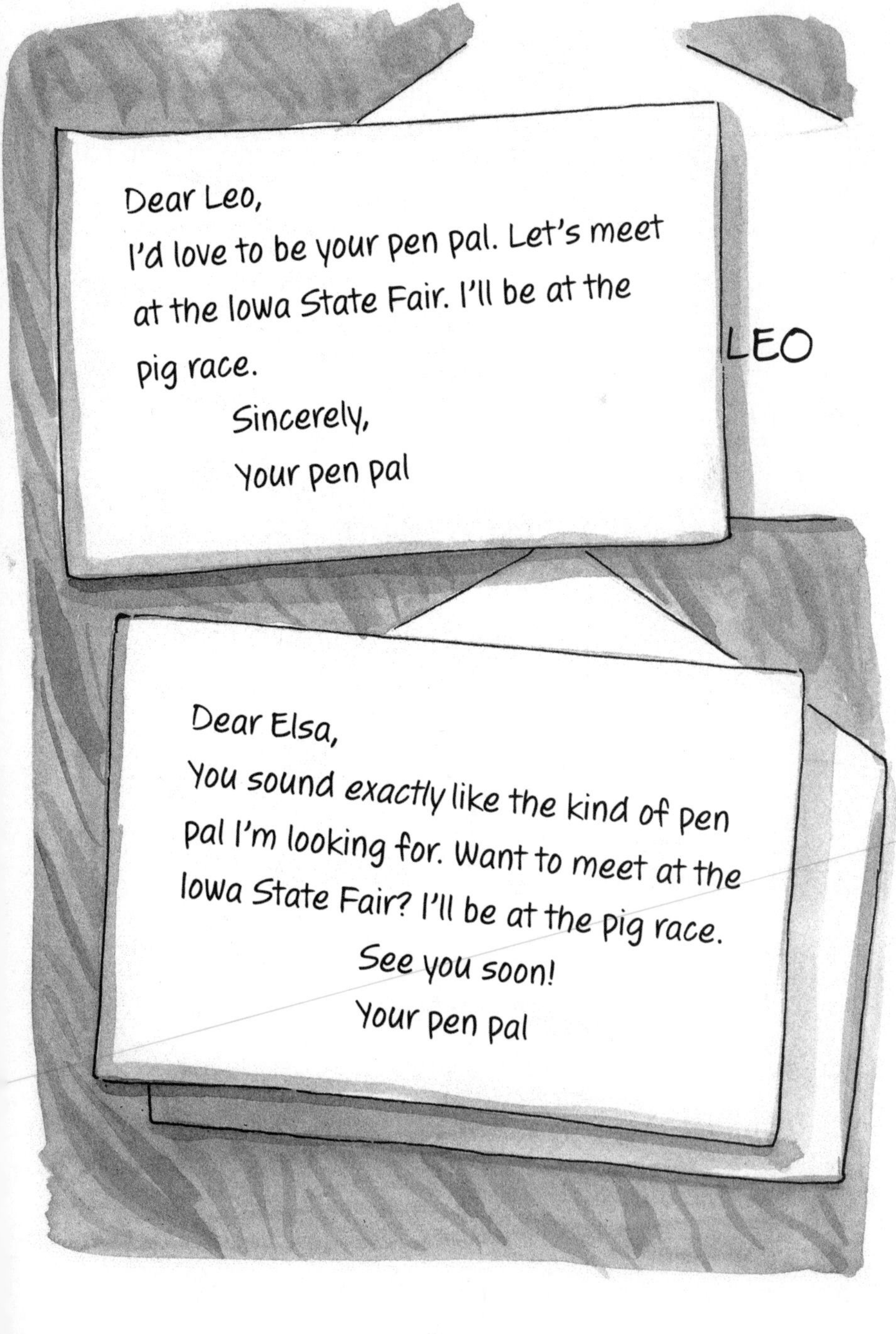

Dear Leo,

I'd love to be your pen pal. Let's meet at the Iowa State Fair. I'll be at the pig race.

Sincerely,
Your pen pal

LEO

Dear Elsa,

You sound exactly like the kind of pen pal I'm looking for. Want to meet at the Iowa State Fair? I'll be at the pig race.

See you soon!
Your pen pal

Bert was disappointed that he didn't receive a letter. He sat under the table with Ruby and pouted.

"I thought for *sure* I'd get a letter today from a pen pal," Bert said. "But what did I get? Nothing."

"If you're in such a big hurry," said Ruby, "make business cards. Pass them out tomorrow at the state fair. You never know who might write to you."

Bert perked up. "That's another great idea! You're smart."

"Thanks," said Ruby. "I like compliments. But do you know what I *really* like?"

"You like chewing things," said Bert. "But you quit, remember?"

"Rats," said Ruby.

❧ CHAPTER FIVE ❧

The Iowa State Fair attracted more than a million visitors every year. People came from all directions. It was the most popular event in the state.

The butter sculpture always drew a big crowd.

Everyone loved the tractor pull.

The tall corn contest was also terrific.

And who could resist the hog-calling contest?

But the most popular event was the annual pig race.
Farmers spent months training their pigs in hopes of
taking home the five-thousand-dollar prize.

At two o'clock on Sunday afternoon, Sir Sidney's Circus arrived at the fair.

The Famous Flying Banana Brothers parked the train on a hill at the edge of the fairgrounds. As everyone climbed off the train, Sir Sidney spoke privately to Ruby.

I noticed you haven't returned any of the things you borrowed.

Because of that, you will remain on the train while the rest of us enjoy the fair.

Pablo watched the other pigs warming up on the track. "I'll never beat those pigs," he whispered to Gert.

"You have to think positive thoughts," Gert replied. "You're the fastest pig alive! Keep telling yourself that."

Farmer Farley was saying the same thing to himself in the locker room as he stuffed pillows into his pig costume. He struggled to zip it up.

Penelope Prinkle arrived at the fair in her *pig*up truck. It had a large scale in the bed. The scale would come in handy if she decided to buy some pigs at the fair.

Bert was busy in the livestock barn, passing out business cards to the horses, cows, goats, and sheep.

Bert heard several people talking in the barn.

"The pig race will begin in five minutes," a man was saying.

"We'd better go to the racetrack now if we want to get a seat," a woman replied.

Bert sprinted to the grandstand and joined the rest of the circus members.

Gert was waving a small flag she had made for the event. "You can do it, Pablo!" she yelled. "I know you can win!"

"Show them what you've got!" added Elsa, who was saving a seat for her pen pal.

Old Coal flew in gentle swoops that spelled out the words

Go Pablo!

Stan and Dan Banana were doing a new trick that made their bodies look like the letter *P*, for *Pablo.*

Leo was getting into the spirit of things, too, with a cheer.

**Pablo, Pablo! He's our pig!
All for Pablo, dance a jig.**

Leo was saving a place for his pen pal, though he wondered how his new best friend would find him in the large and noisy crowd.

Sir Sidney sat quietly on the bleachers, thinking about Ruby. He wondered if he'd been too hard on the pack rat, making her stay behind on the train while everyone else enjoyed the fair. He decided he would do some research on pack rats after the pig race.

The pigs were called to the starting line. Farmer Farley took his place near the center of the track. Pablo was in the outside lane. They didn't see each other because they were too busy worrying about the race.

The judge explained the rules. "I expect all pigs to be on their best behavior," she said. "There will be no pushing, tripping, scratching, or biting other pigs. You will run one lap around the track. The first pig to cross the finish line will be declared the winner.

Now, on your mark.

Get set.

GO!"

"Oh, isn't this exciting?" Gert said. She offered Bert an extra flag. "You can show your support for Pablo by waving this flag. That is, if you *want* him to win."

"Of course I want Pablo to win," Bert grumped.

"Pablo thinks you don't like him," Gert said.

"I like Pablo just fine," Bert said. "I just don't like that *you* have a pen pal and I don't. But that will soon change." He handed Gert one of his business cards.

Gert tucked the card into her pocket. Then she raised her voice and cheered for her friend.

Come on, Pablo! You can do it! Run, pen pal, run!

Bert couldn't see the racetrack. A tall woman in a fancy hat was sitting in front of him. To get a better view, Bert climbed higher in the grandstand. He reached the very top and sneaked into the broadcasting booth. An announcer was describing the race for fans listening on the radio.

"What a race, folks! The pigs are snout to snout on the straightaway. It's Sassy Sausage by a whisker. But here comes Almost Bacon! He's running like his life depends on this, and it probably does. Now here's Muddy Mama. And look at Pablo! He's no slow pork. This is going to be a close race, friends. Hey, check out Fat Chance! He sure is a fast one. That piggy's going to market!"

Bert had found the best seat at the racetrack. "Come on, Pablo," he cheered quietly. He didn't want to get kicked out of the booth. The announcer was fun to watch.

"They're almost halfway around the track now," the announcer said. "All these pigs look strong. No pickled pigs' feet here. Anyone could win, but Sassy Sausage sure looks tasty. At the halfway mark, it's Sassy Sausage in front, Pablo in second, and Fat Chance right behind."

Pablo and Farmer Farley were both running as fast as they could. They still hadn't seen each other. But as they rounded the bend, Pablo caught a glimpse of Farmer Farley, whose pig costume was beginning to rip.

Farmer Farley didn't notice Pablo. He was too busy thinking about his farm and how desperately he needed to win the prize money. He picked up his pace and was soon neck and neck with Pablo. That's when he turned his head slightly and saw a familiar face.

Farmer Farley's pig suit now had a big rip, but he kept running. So did Pablo. They could see the finish line in front of them.

"We're in the homestretch now," said the announcer. "It's still Sassy Sausage in front, with Pablo behind her and Fat Chance in third.

But wait! Pablo is picking up steam. He's pulling ahead of Sassy Sausage.

And here comes Fat Chance. Pablo is ahead of Sassy Sausage. Now Fat Chance is snout to snout with Pablo! It's going to be close, folks! Who will bring home the bacon?"

"Go, Pablo, go!" Gert yelled from the stands.

But Pablo couldn't hear Gert. He was too distracted by the pig running next to him. Where had he seen those eyes?

Farmer Farley kept glancing over at Pablo. *How strange,* Farmer Farley thought. *That pig looks exactly like . . .*

Sassy Sausage took the opportunity to speed in front of Pablo and Farmer Farley, just before they crossed the finish line.

"It's Sassy Sausage in first place!" called the radio announcer. "Pablo and Fat Chance are tangled up in second place. Somebody better call the *ham*bulance."

❧ CHAPTER SIX ❧

Pablo and Farmer Farley were not badly hurt.

But they were in *big* trouble, because Penelope Prinkle had seen the whole thing, including the moment Farmer Farley climbed out of his torn pig suit. She came running from the grandstand as fast as a greased pig.

"Well, well, well," she said when she reached Pablo and Farmer Farley. "What a surprise to see you both here. And look at the time! It's three o'clock on the dot." She turned to Farmer Farley. "That means you owe me five thousand dollars."

Farmer Farley's eyes filled with tears. He hated the idea of selling his only pig. But now that Farmer Farley had lost the race, how else could he possibly come up with the five thousand dollars he needed to pay Penelope Prinkle?

"Here," Farmer Farley said sadly, surrendering Pablo to Penelope Prinkle. "He means the world to me. To you, he's worth only five thousand dollars."

"Not unless he weighs five hundred pounds," Penelope Prinkle said with an evil grin.

She led the way to her *pig*up truck.

"Climb onto the scale," she ordered.

Pablo did as he was told.

Penelope Prinkle used a pen and paper to quickly calculate what she owed Farmer Farley.

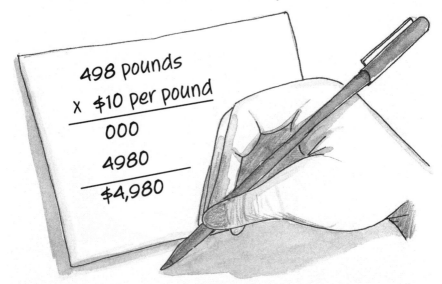

498 pounds
x $10 per pound
000
4980
$4,980

"Here's four thousand nine hundred and eighty dollars," she said, counting out the money.

"But I need five thousand dollars to repay my loan," said Farmer Farley.

"Too bad," said Penelope Prinkle. "Now I own your pig *and* your land."

Sir Sidney spoke up. "Please, Ms. Prinkle, let me give you five thousand dollars to spare Pablo's life and save Farmer Farley's land."

"No, thank you," Penelope Prinkle said. "Come on, Pablo. It's back to the pork chop factory for you."

Good-bye, Gert.

Oh, Pablo!

Bert was watching the sad scene from the announcer's booth. Sure, he was jealous that Gert had a pen pal. But he didn't want Pablo to end up on somebody's plate as a pork chop dinner.

"Poor Pablo," Bert said to himself. "Poor Gert."

"Huh?" said the radio announcer. "Who was that?"

"Just me," said Bert.

"Ack! I hate mice!" The announcer grabbed a broom and began chasing Bert around the booth, swatting at him angrily.

Bert tried to escape by scampering up a file cabinet and hiding. He wished someone would help him, but all his friends were down below with Pablo. Bert looked out the window. That's when he saw it.

The circus train was slowly rolling toward the racetrack.

"Holy train wreck!" Bert cried. "Look at that!"

"Oh, no you don't," said the announcer. "I'm not going to be distracted by a little birdie out the window."

"This is no birdie," said Bert. "It's a runaway circus train. Look!"

The announcer grabbed his microphone and began calling the play-by-play action.

"Breaking news here at the pig race! Sir Sidney's Circus train is rolling toward a crowd of people and pigs gathered on the racetrack. Folks, this is a runaway train!"

"There's a rat on the train but nobody else," the announcer repeated.

"The train's going to run over everyone on the track!" Bert said.

"The train's going to run over everyone on the track!" the announcer repeated.

"No one below can hear you," Bert said.

"No one below can hear—"

The announcer stopped repeating Bert's exact words. "You're right! Only the radio fans can hear me."

"We've got to warn Sir Sidney and the others," Bert said, pounding his tiny paws on the glass that encased the booth.

"There's a switch around here somewhere," said the announcer, fumbling with knobs on the control panel. "I should be able to turn on the speakers in the fairgrounds."

The train was picking up speed as it rolled down the hill. Bert couldn't wait a second longer. He dashed out of the booth and yelled from the top of his lungs.

Look out, everyone!

Gert heard her brother's warning. "Good grief!" she said when she saw the train. "Move quickly, everyone! The circus train is headed our way."

Sir Sidney and the circus members ran to safety. Farmer Farley also moved quickly out of the way.

But Penelope Prinkle didn't hear Bert's warning or see everyone running. She was too busy trying to get Pablo to stop crying. Pablo's eyes were too wet with tears to see what was happening.

Pablo's ears perked up. He blinked back his tears.
That's when he saw the speeding train headed right for
Penelope Prinkle
and him.

At the same moment, the radio announcer flipped the switch that turned on the fairground speakers. "Can you hear me, folks? Heavens to bacon, have we got a mess over here at the racetrack! A speeding train is heading straight toward a pig named Pablo and the princess of pork, Penelope Prinkle. This is bad, folks. Really bad."

The announcer paused to take a sip of water.

"But wait!" he continued. "What's this? The pig is flexing his muscles. Now he's . . . Can he possibly do this? He's stepping in front of Ms. Prinkle. It looks like . . . Is he really going to attempt to stop the train? People are running from all over the fairgrounds to see this. Never in my life did I think I'd see such pigheaded foolishness. Don't try this at home, kids! The pig can't possibly stop a moving train with his bare hooves. Can he? Here comes the train!"

Pablo made the front page of the evening edition of the *New Pork Times*.

𝕿𝖍𝖊 𝕹𝖊𝖜 𝕻𝖔𝖗𝖐 𝕿𝖎𝖒𝖊𝖘

"All the pork that's fit to print with news that's never *boar*ing"

Sunday, August 17 ✦ **50 cents** ✦ **Evening Edition**

Pork Chop Bigwig Saved by Brave Pig

Pig stops runaway train.

Call him brave or call him crazy. One thing is certain: Pablo the pig saved Penelope Prinkle's life earlier today when he stopped a runaway train from crushing her to death.

"I knew Pablo was strong," said Farmer Farley. "But I never thought he could stop a moving train with his bare hooves."

"It must have been his secret strength shining through," said Gert, a circus mouse and Pablo's pen pal. The pig and mouse became friends last year after writing letters to the Pen Pal Shop.

No one was seriously injured by the train, though Penelope Prinkle suffered a broken nose after tripping over her boots. Luckily, the *ham*bulance crew was on hand to provide medical care.

"My nose may never be the same," said Penelope Prinkle. "But that's okay. After this experience, I don't feel like the same person on the inside, either. I've had a change of heart, thanks to Pablo."

Farley and Prinkle Plan a Merger

Remember the $5,000 Farmer Farley owed Penelope Prinkle? Well, forget about it.

"I don't want to take Farmer Farley's money or his land," said Penelope Prinkle. "I want only his cooperation. We will work together to combine our properties and form a new business that will benefit the entire pig community, including Pablo, who risked his life to save mine."

When he learned he could keep his pig and his land, Farmer Farley turned a cartwheel. "This is the best

Fred Farley and
Penelope Prinkle will be partners.

day ever!" he said.

Penelope Prinkle agreed. "I'm so happy to be alive," she said. "I'm going to shred my notebook of debts and start a new chapter in my life."

Pack Rat Caused Runaway Train

Investigators with the Iowa State Fair have determined the cause of the runaway circus train that came close to killing Penelope Prinkle this afternoon. A pack rat named Ruby chewed through the train's electrical wires, causing the parking brake to fail.

"I tried to give up chewing, but I couldn't," said Ruby. "I'm a pack rat. I was born to chew." Then she fled the scene.

The owner of the circus train, Sir Sidney, offered to pay for any damages caused by the rat's behavior. "I will take responsibility," he said. "It's partly my fault for insisting Ruby stay on the train."

Ruby makes no apology.

Sir Sidney explained he'd never met a pack rat until Ruby arrived on his circus train. "But I've done some research on pack rats," he said. "I've learned we can't blame them for chewing things. They do it keep their teeth healthy, just like pigs roll in the mud to keep cool. We shouldn't criticize anyone until we've walked a mile in his hooves or lived an hour in her fur."

≥ CHAPTER SEVEN ≤

The next week, Iowa farmers were back in their fields, harvesting sweet corn.

They made butter, drove tractors, and called hogs.

On Saturday afternoon, after they'd finished all their chores, the farmers drove their pigs to the land now shared by Penelope Prinkle and Farmer Farley.

The former headquarters of Prinkle's Pork Chops was now a theme park for farmers, pigs, and all creatures great and small. They came from miles away to enjoy the rides and wander happily through the maze Farmer Farley had created in his cornfield.

Sir Sidney's Circus arrived by train on opening day to put on a free show for all the pigs and farmers. Gert performed a duet with her special guest, Pablo.

(Sing to the tune of "I've Been Working on the Railroad")

I've been writing to my pen pal,
All the live long day.
I've been writing to my pen pal,
Just because I want to say:
You sure write a lovely letter.
Makes me so proud to be your friend.
I will always be your pen pal.
This is not the end.

(Chorus)
Pen pal, won't you write?
Pen pal, won't you write?
Pen pal, won't you write to me-e-e?
Pen pal, won't you write,
Pen pal, won't you write,
Pen pal, won't you write to me?

Everybody needs a pen pal.
Everybody needs a friend to write to.
Everybody needs a pen pal.
Maybe I can write to you!

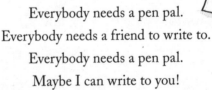

Me, my, piggly-i-o
Me, my, piggly-i-o-o-o-o
Me, my, piggly-i-o
Writing to the pal I know.

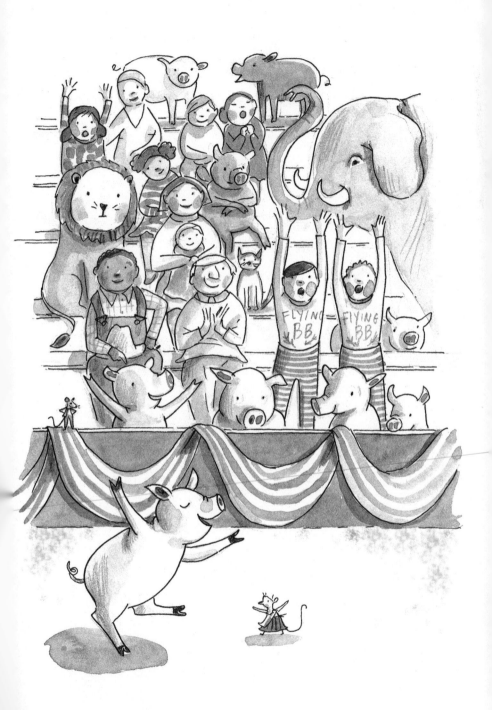

It was a fun and silly song, but it made some listeners feel a little sad. Leo and Elsa hadn't found their pen pals at the pig race. Bert hadn't even *heard* from his pen pal.

After the song, Pablo performed a weight-lifting demonstration. The crowd went hog wild when he held Elsa over his head.

Hooray!

Other pigs had special talents they wanted to show off, too. One pig named Placido yodeled. Two pigs named Peaches and Plum juggled fruit while calling their farmers.

Another pig named Presley played the banjo.

One clever pig named Plato even rode a bicycle.

A few pigs hadn't yet found their talent. So the Banana brothers gave lessons in tightrope walking.

Elsa held a class in tango dancing.

And Leo and Tiger taught four pigs how to sing together in perfect harmony.

Penelope Prinkle watched all this from the comfort of her old office, which she had converted into a skybox. She and Sir Sidney sat together, laughing and eating popcorn.

"I think your Pig Palace and Theme Park will be a big success," Sir Sidney said. "But you might not make as much money as you did selling pork chops."

"Oh, I don't care about that," said Penelope Prinkle. "This is so much more fun. Do you want to know a secret, Sir Sidney?"

Sir Sidney raised his eyebrows. "Maybe. What is your secret?"

"Making pigs happy," Penelope Prinkle whispered, "is even *more* fun than making money."

Leo and Elsa had fun, too, when Old Coal delivered a letter to each of them from the Pen Pal Shop. They opened and read their letters separately.

Dear Leo,

I'm so sorry I missed you at the pig race! I hope to see you at the Pig Palace. Let's meet at three o'clock under the clock.

Your pen pal

Dear Elsa,

I can't wait to finally see you face-to-face! Can you be at the Pig Palace at 3:00 today? I'll meet you under the clock.

Your pen pal

"I'm so excited to finally meet my pen pal," Leo said.

"Me, too," said Elsa. "My pen pal sounds so nice. I'm sure he'll never say anything to hurt my feelings."

"My pen pal will never call me disgusting," said Leo.

They were both remembering their recent fight.

"Leo," said Elsa softly, "I didn't mean *you* were disgusting. I was talking about fleas. But even fleas aren't disgusting. They have a job to do, just like all of us. Oh, Leo. I'm so sorry if I hurt your feelings."

"I'm sorry, too," said Leo. "I didn't mean to upset you by mentioning your weight. I love how big you are. I'd never do anything to hurt your feelings on purpose."

"I believe you," said Elsa. "You were a wonderful friend."

They stood in silence for a minute, unable to think of any words that could fix their broken friendship.

"My pen pal is meeting me here at three o'clock," said Leo.

"*My* pen pal is meeting *me* here at three o'clock," said Elsa.

They looked up at the clock on top of the Pig Palace. It was exactly three o'clock.

Leo and Elsa laughed until they cried.

"But wait," said Elsa, looking at Leo's letter from his pen pal. "I didn't write that letter to you."

"I didn't write to you, either," said Leo. "I just sent a letter to the Pen Pal Shop, asking for a new best friend."

"I agree," said Elsa. She curled her trunk around Leo's shoulders. Then the two friends hugged tightly. They were too busy hugging to notice Old Coal fly by with a pen in her beak.

The circus crow had a secret of her own.

❧ CHAPTER EIGHT ❧

It was hard for Gert and Pablo to say good-bye.

Will you write to me?

Of course! I'll write to you *dappily*.

daily + happily = dappily

They waved as the circus train departed for its next destination.

Later that morning, Sir Sidney cooked a healthful brunch for his friends. Everyone enjoyed the scrambled eggs, whole wheat toast, kale chips, and fresh yogurt with blueberries.

"I've also cooked up a training program for us,"
Sir Sidney said. "I think we'll all feel better if we follow
these simple guidelines."

SIR SIDNEY'S CIRCUS TRAINING PROGRAM

DIET
Protein
Healthy fats
Fruits and vegetables
Whole grains

SLEEP
Nine hours every night

EXERCISE THE BODY
Run one mile.
Lift light weights.

EXERCISE THE MIND
Read for pleasure thirty
minutes every night.

Sir Sidney smiled. "The other day we were talking about the secrets we hide from each other. But did you know that you all have secret talents that might be hidden from *you*? One of your jobs as you get older is to try to discover what your secret strengths and talents are. Maybe Leo has a special gift for yodeling. Elsa, you might be a natural on a bicycle. You'll have to try lots of different things before you discover your hidden gift."

"Your secret strength is what you were born to do," said Sir Sidney. "You'll know you've found it when you're doing something that makes the world a better place."

"Ruby's secret strength must've been chewing," said Elsa.

"You're right," said Leo. "If Ruby hadn't chewed through the wires on the train, Pablo wouldn't have had the opportunity to save Penelope Prinkle's life, which in turn saved his own life. That led to the creation of Prinkle's Pig Palace and Theme Park."

"Isn't it *wonderful* when everything turns out for the best?" said Elsa.

"Harrumph," muttered Bert. He was listening to all this from under the table. He still hadn't received a letter from anyone who wanted to be his pen pal. To make matters worse, now that Ruby was gone, Bert didn't have anyone to complain to. He shuffled back to the mouse hole, feeling depressed and lonely.

Gert helped Sir Sidney clean up the brunch dishes.

"Thank you for sharing your secret with us," Sir Sidney said to Gert.

"You're not mad that I have a pig for a pen pal?" asked Gert.

"Of course not," said Sir Sidney. "But I was talking about your *other* secret."

Gert was confused. "What other secret do I have?"

Sir Sidney bent over and picked up Gert. He placed her in the palm of his hand.

You have a secret strength for being the best friend any pig could ever have.

Do you think so?

"I *know* so," said Sir Sidney, returning Gert to the table. "And being a good friend doesn't mean you can't also be a good sister."

Gert nibbled her claws. She had spent so much time worrying about Pablo, she had almost forgotten about her brother. She remembered the little card Bert had given her at the pig race. She pulled it out of her pocket and read it.

Bert the Circus Mouse
I'm looking for a pen pal.
Write to me in care of
Sir Sidney's Circus train.

Gert smiled after reading the card. Then she grabbed a notepad and pencil and began to write a letter to her brother.

Thirty minutes later when Gert returned to the mouse hole to deliver her letter, she found her brother surrounded by mail.

There must have been more than a hundred cards and letters, all for Bert.

"If you want everyone to be your pen pal," said Gert, "you'll have to write a letter to each and every new friend."

"Do you realize how *long* it would take me to write back to *all* these pen pals?" asked Bert. "It would take a whole *year*. Besides, I don't have my favorite pen. Ruby never gave it back to me."

Gert listened to her brother's excuses. Then she made a suggestion. "Why don't you pick one letter from the pile? You can find time to write to *one* new friend. That could be your pen pal."

Bert closed his eyes and pulled an envelope from the pile. He opened it and read the letter to himself.

RUBY
Professional Pack Rat

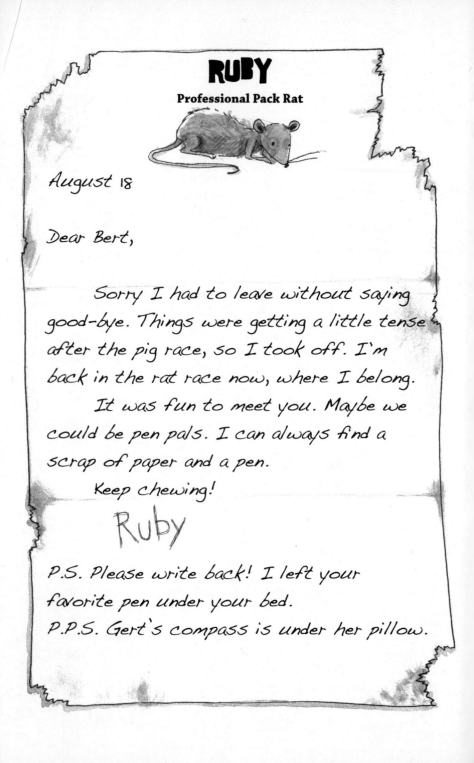

August 18

Dear Bert,

Sorry I had to leave without saying good-bye. Things were getting a little tense after the pig race, so I took off. I'm back in the rat race now, where I belong.

It was fun to meet you. Maybe we could be pen pals. I can always find a scrap of paper and a pen.

Keep chewing!

Ruby

P.S. Please write back! I left your favorite pen under your bed.

P.P.S. Gert's compass is under her pillow.

Bert found his favorite pen. Then he sat down to write a letter to Ruby.

Elsa and Leo also became pen pals. They wrote letters to each other every day.

LEO THE LION
Proud Member of Sir Sidney's Circus

August 24

Dear Elsa,

I like you just the way you are.

Leo

From the Desk of Elsa

August 24

Dear Leo,

I feel exactly the same about you. I hope we'll always be best friends.
Elsa

They also exchanged gifts.

Elsa and Leo didn't ask Old Coal to deliver their letters or gifts, which was lucky. The crow was busy with other mail. Thanks to all the recent publicity, her business had become wildly popular with animals all over the world.

PEN PAL SHOP
P.O. Box 744
Mountain Grove, MO
65711

No one knew that Old Coal was the mastermind behind the Pen Pal Shop. No one guessed she had a hidden talent for finding and fixing friendships.

That was Old Coal's secret.

ABOUT THE AUTHOR AND ILLUSTRATOR

KATE KLISE and **M. SARAH KLISE** are sisters who like to write (Kate) and draw (Sarah). They began making books when they were little girls who shared a bedroom in Peoria, Illinois. Kate now lives and writes in an old farmhouse on forty acres in the Missouri Ozarks. Sarah draws and dwells in a Victorian cottage in Berkeley, California. Together the Klise sisters have created more than twenty award-winning books for young readers. Their goal always is to make the kind of fun-to-read books they loved years ago when they were kids.

To learn more about the Klise sisters, visit their website: www.kateandsarahklise.com.

You might also enjoy visiting Sir Sidney and his friends at www.threeringrascals.com.